MARLENE'S MAGIC

☆ BIRTHDAY ☆

To Elaine
AL

This edition published in 1998 by
Diamond Books
77-85 Fulham Palace Road
Hammersmith, London

First published in Picture Lions 1993
Picture Lions is an imprint of the Children's Division,
part of HarperCollins Publishers Ltd

ISBN 0 261 66952 4

Printed and bound in Slovenia

MARLENE'S MAGIC

☆ BIRTHDAY ☆

Antony Lishak

Illustrated by Sami Sweeten

CARNIVAL

It was Marlene's birthday. All her friends
were coming over so she was helping to
get things ready.

A van pulled up outside.

"Who's the birthday boy then?" asked the van driver as he brought in the cake.

"I am!" said Marlene as she went upstairs to change.

Marlene looked great in her witch costume.

But no one else knew it was a fancy dress party.

Everyone brought Marlene a birthday present.

"Robots, thanks," she said. "Just what I wanted!"

Then the music started.

But Marlene and her friends weren't
interested in dancing.

"Tea time!" said Marlene's mum.

Marlene passed around the tea cakes.
Daniel frisbied doughnuts, Emily scoffed
sandwiches and Adam sloshed jelly down
Gemma's back.

Marlene drank orange juice through a straw.
Alex gargled milkshake, Samantha slurped squash

and Gregory gulped so much lemonade that he got the hiccups.

Then they played 'Pin the tail on the donkey'.

"Me first!" said Gemma, but she missed.

Marlene's dog Toby joined in 'Pass the parcel'.

He wasn't sure of the rules!

Marlene was relieved when the magician
was ready.

She was looking forward to this.

First, he tried to produce a rabbit from inside his top hat.

"Look behind you!" everyone shouted.

Then he made a newspaper cone and poured
in some water.

And for his next trick…

he almost made Marlene disappear.

Finally, the magician packed his things away
and everyone thought he had finished.

"Marlene, time to cut the cake," called
her mum.

But he saved his best trick till the end!